THE ADVENTURES OF
Vallorie and Ashley

The First Day of School

TRACY RICHARDSON

Fulton Books, Inc.
Meadville, PA

First originally published by Fulton Books 2016

ISBN 978-1-63338-275-6 (Paperback)
ISBN 978-1-63338-276-3 (Digital)

Printed in the United States of America

THE ADVENTURES OF
Vallorie and Ashley

It's the first day of school.
The little girls want to look their best.
"It's hard to choose," the girls say as they
rumble through their closets.

"It's time for school," yells Bubbles.
There is so much to do.
The girls are excited to go to school to
talk about their summer vacation.

The bell rings.

Ashley loves math. "That's my favorite class. I love adding and subtracting. I like to count. I can count up to one hundred."

"I love reading and writing," Vallorie says. "I love to curl up in the bed on a rainy day and read a good book. One day I'm going to be a writer."

8

It's time for lunch. The girls meet up in the lunch room. They talk and eat.

"It's always fun to share with friends," says Vallorie.

13

After lunch, the girls go to gym.
In gym class, they jump rope.
Ashley counts 1, 2, 3, as Vallorie
turns the rope.

After gym class, Vallorie and Ashley go to recess and practice for dance class. The dance instructor is planning a school dance.

The girls really have moves! They really know how to dance.

"This dance is going to be the best dance in school history," says Vallorie.

"Yes, it is. This is the best first day of school ever," says Ashley.

The End

ABOUT THE AUTHOR

Tracy Richardson resides on the west side of Detroit, Michigan. She was raised by her grandmother. She is a proud parent of ten children and a grandmother of three.

CPSIA information can be obtained
at www.ICGtesting.com
Printed in the USA
BVHW02s2354030818
523540BV00006B/10/P

9 781633 382756